To my father, whose gentleness and humor and ready supply of bedtime stories
(especially those involving Skitty the Kitty) are where it all began —E. T.

For Allyn Johnston and Rubin Pfeffer,
who know about bears and scarecrows —L. S.

With special thanks to Bethany Hegedus and The Writing Barn for bringing us all together

BEACH LANE BOOKS

An imprint of Simon & Schuster Children's Publishing Division

1230 Avenue of the Americas, New York, New York 10020

Text copyright © 2020 by Ellen Tarlow

Illustrations copyright © 2020 by Lauren Stringer

All rights reserved, including the right of reproduction in whole or in part in any form.

BEACH LANE BOOKS is a trademark of Simon & Schuster, Inc.

For information about special discounts for bulk purchases, please contact Simon & Schuster Special Sales at 1-866-506-1949 or business@simonandschuster.com.

The Simon & Schuster Speakers Bureau can bring authors to your live event. For more information or to book an event, contact the Simon & Schuster Speakers Bureau at 1-866-248-3049 or visit our website at www.simonspeakers.com.

Book design by Lauren Stringer and Karyn Lee

The text for this book was set in Adobe Caslon Pro.

The illustrations for this book were rendered in watercolor, gouache, and acrylic on Arches oil paper.

Manufactured in China • 0720 SCP

First Edition

10 9 8 7 6 5 4 3 2 1

Library of Congress Cataloging-in-Publication Data • Names: Tarlow, Ellen, author. | Stringer, Lauren, illustrator. • Title: Looking for Smile / Ellen Tarlow ; illustrated by Lauren Stringer. • Description: First edition. | New York : Beach Lane Books, [2020] | Audience: Ages 4-8. | Audience: Grades 2-3. | Summary: "What is Bear to do when he wakes up one day to find his Smile gone?"— Provided by publisher. • Identifiers: LCCN 2019055461 (print) | LCCN 2019055462 (ebook) | ISBN 9781534466197 (hardcover) | ISBN 9781534466203 (ebook) • Subjects: CYAC: Smiling—Fiction. | Lost and found possessions—Fiction. | Bears—Fiction. • Classification: LCC PZ7.T174 Loo 2020 (print) | LCC PZ7.T174 (ebook) | DDC [E]—dc23 • LC record available at https://lccn.loc.gov/2019055461 • LC ebook record available at https://lccn.loc.gov/2019055462

Looking for Smile

Ellen Tarlow   Lauren Stringer

Beach Lane Books
New York London Toronto Sydney New Delhi

Bear and Smile were always together.

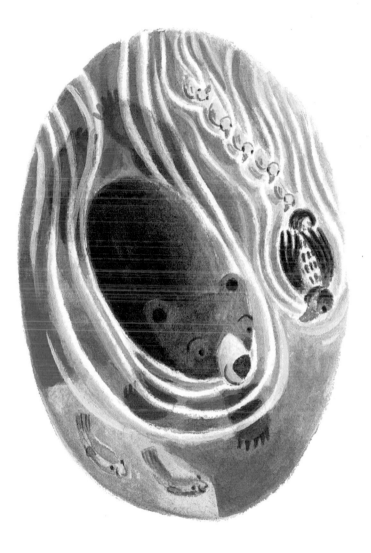

In the mornings, Bear woke up and stretched out wide across his bed.

Smile woke up too and stretched out wide across Bear's face.
"Good morning," said Bear.

Bear and Smile liked all the same things.
bear liked nuts and berries best for breakfast.
That's what Smile liked best too.
(They shared them together perfectly.)

Together they went to the most wonderful places.

"Waterfall!" cried Bear, jumping in.

It took Smile a few minutes to catch up.
(Longer if the water was extra cold.)
But then they splashed together for hours.

Bear and Smile loved adventures.
(As long as they weren't too scary.)

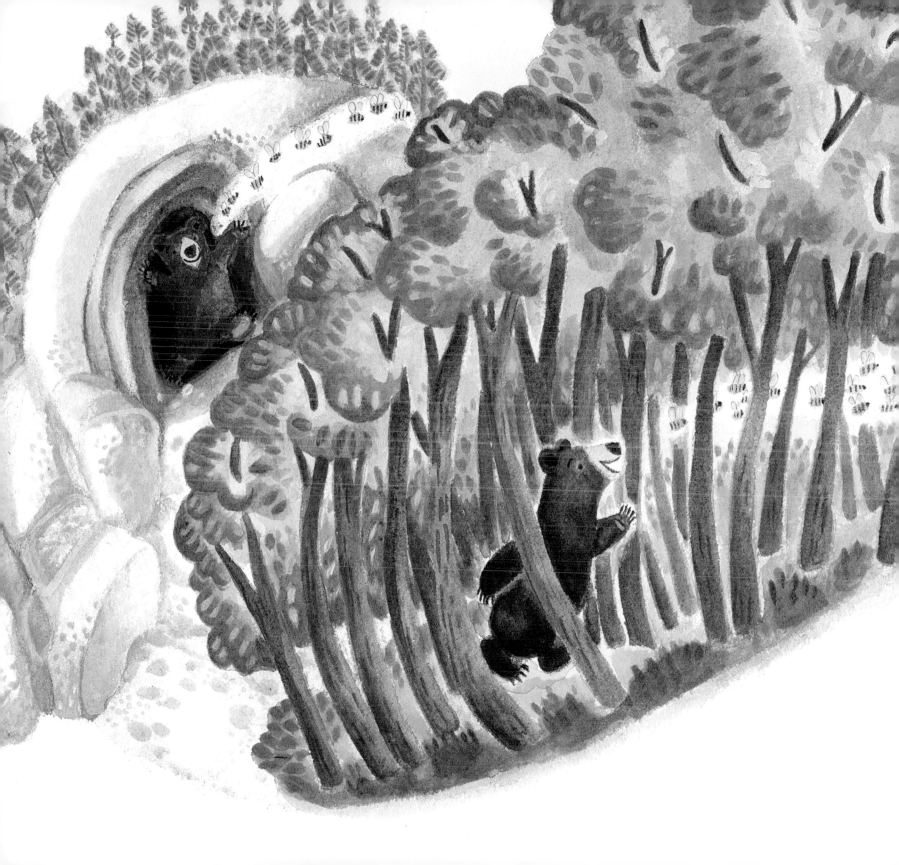

They would do almost anything for honey.
(Though Smile usually waited until
the bees were out of sight.)

Always together, Bear and Smile.

Then one morning, Smile didn't come.

"Smile!" Bear called. "It's time to wake up!"

He waited.

"Smile!" he called. "It's time for breakfast!"

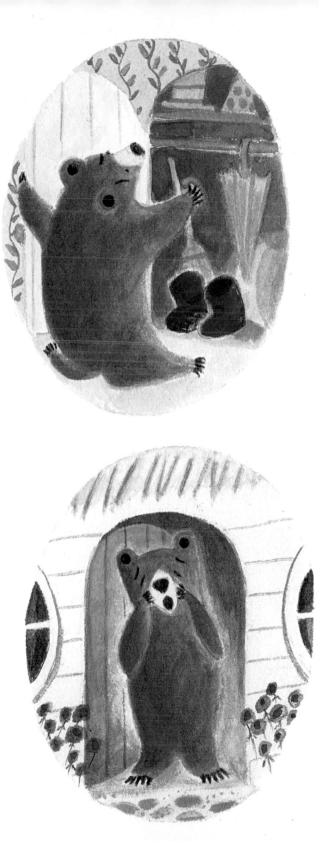

But Smile didn't come for breakfast.
And Bear noticed that nuts and berries didn't
taste as good without his friend.

Bear looked under the bed.
He looked in the closet.
He opened the door.
"Smile!" he called. "Where are you?"

"Hello, Bear," said Rabbit. "What's the matter? You look different."

"I lost Smile," said Bear.

"Oh, dear," said Rabbit. "Did you look in your favorite places?"

"Oh!" said Bear. "Good thinking."

He ran right to the waterfall.

"Smile!" he called. "It's me, Bear!"

He jumped in.

He splashed the way Smile liked best.

But Smile didn't come to splash.

Bear looked up.

He looked down.

He looked inside.

He looked outside.

"I know," said Bear at last. "Smile *always* wants honey."

Bear got a pawful.

He sat beneath the tree and ate.

But Smile didn't come to take a bite.

Bear sighed.
The day was gray.
The woods seemed empty.

"What's wrong, Bear?" asked a voice.
It was Bird.
"I lost Smile," said Bear.

"Oh, poor Bear," said Bird, and she sat down
right next to her friend.

The two sat, not saying a word.

Then Bird began to sing quietly.

And Bear began to hum.

Together they sang and hummed and
looked out at the swirling leaves.

Then Bear felt something
deep inside him.

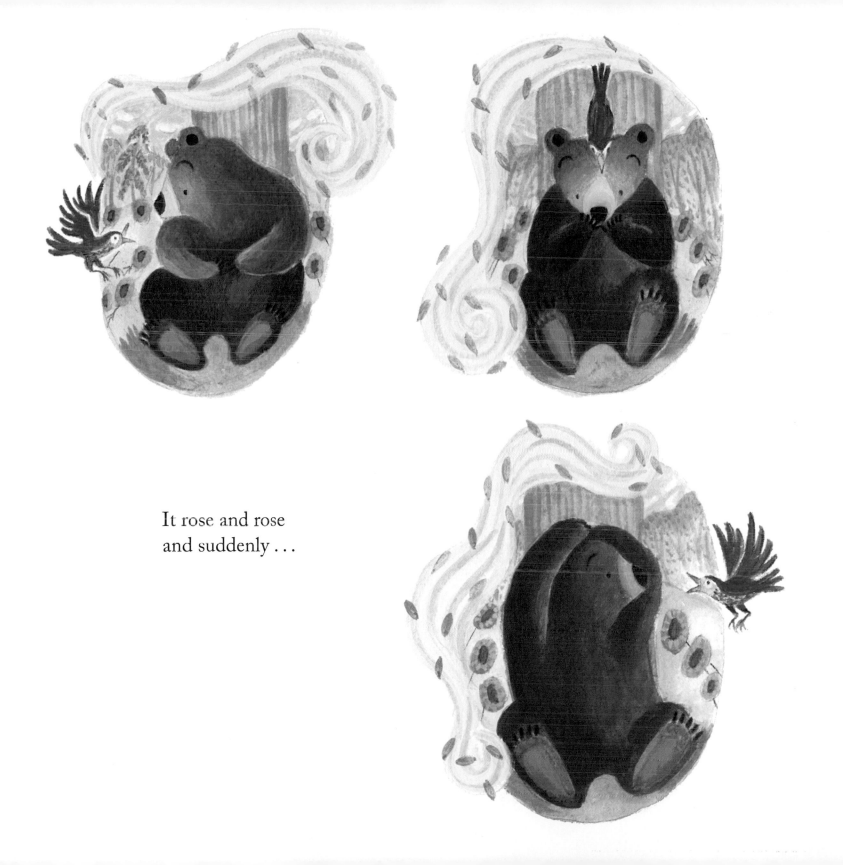

It rose and rose
and suddenly . . .

there was Smile!

"Hello," said Bear. "I missed you."
And what did Smile do then?

Smile smiled.